Editor: Nicole Lanctot
Production manager: Louise Kurtz
Designer: Ada Rodriguez

First published in the United States of America in 2015 by Abbeville Press,
137 Varick Street, New York, NY 10013

First published in Belgium in 2015 by Editions Mijade,
18, rue de l'ouvrage, 5000 Namur

First edition
10 9 8 7 6 5 4 3 2 1

ISBN 978-0-7892-1244-3

Library of Congress Cataloging-in-Publication Data available upon request

For bulk and premium sales and for text adoption procedures, write to Customer
Service Manager, Abbeville Press, 137 Varick Street, New York, NY 10013,
or call 1-800-ARTBOOK.

Visit Abbeville Press online at www.abbeville.com.

Ping and Pong
the Penguins

Sylviane Gangloff

Abbeville Kids
A DIVISION OF ABBEVILLE PRESS
New York · London

Hello! My name is Ping. I'm a penguin.

Hello! I'm a penguin. My name is Pong.

Hey, you! Over there!

Oh! Another penguin.

What are you doing in my book?

Excuse me,
but this is my book!

Will you please get out of here!

Out of the question! Will *you* please get out of here?

Grrr...

Humph...

Oh!

Hey, who's that?

You, over there! Please erase that penguin.

Whoa, there!

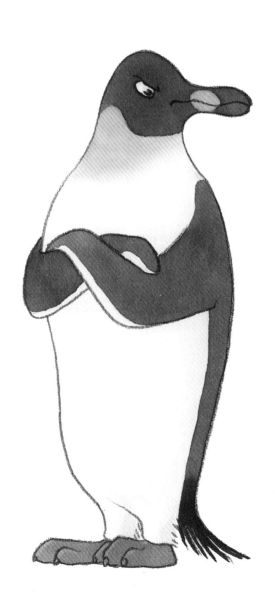

No! Stop!
Erase that one!

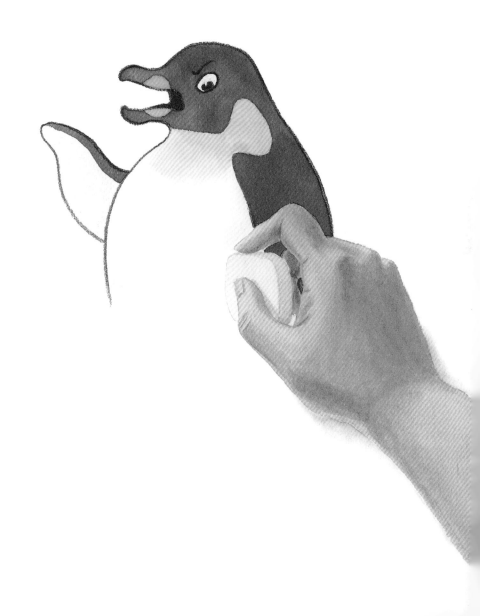

Look what you've done to me!

What about me?

We're not looking too good here…

What's this?

What's he doing now?

Now, that's nice!

Don't forget me!

Phew, that's better!

Oh, thank you!

I have an idea…

This is fun. Tra la la…

Hum hum hum…

Hey, I can draw, too.

Tra la la hum hum…

Hum hum tra la la…

You draw so well!

So do you!

If you like, you can stay in my book!

If you like, you can stay in my book, too!